For Annelise Katherine Edelman & Devin Emery Hessler
—C.G.

To baby Luca, when he finally took a nap
—L.E.

WAAAAAAAAAAA

Text copyright © 2020 by Chris Grabenstein
Jacket art and interior illustrations copyright © 2020 by Leo Espinosa

All rights reserved. Published in the United States by Random House Children's Books,
a division of Penguin Random House LLC, New York.

Random House and the colophon are registered trademarks of Penguin Random House LLC.

Visit us on the Web! rhcbooks.com

Educators and librarians, for a variety of teaching tools, visit us at RHTeachersLibrarians.com

Library of Congress Cataloging-in-Publication Data is available upon request.
ISBN 978-1-5247-7128-7 (trade) — ISBN 978-1-5247-7129-4 (lib. bdg.) — ISBN 978-1-5247-7130-0 (ebook)

Book design by Nicole de las Heras

MANUFACTURED IN CHINA
10 9 8 7 6 5 4 3 2 1
First Edition

JJ
GRABENSTEIN
CHRIS

No More Naps!

A Story for When You're Wide-Awake
and Definitely NOT Tired

Chris Grabenstein   pictures by Leo Espinosa

Random House 🏠 New York

Annalise Devin McFleece did not want to take a nap.

She would fuss.

She would fume.

She would scream.

She would

But she would not ever—no, NEVER—
take a nap.
(Do *you* know anyone like that?)

"You're tired," said her mother.

"You're cranky," crooned her father.

"You're m-m-making my c-c-cakes c-c-crumble," worried the baker downstairs.

"I've never heard anything so loud!" shouted the construction workers breaking up concrete on the sidewalk.

But it didn't matter what her parents or the baker or the construction workers or anybody said.

Do you think Annalise Devin McFleece would take a nap?

No! She would not.
So her father plotted the perfect plan.
"Let's go for a stroll. That will surely
make you sleepy!"

Outside, the sun was warm.
Annalise's stroller rocked. It rolled.
"Sleepy?" asked her father with a
great big yawn.

Annalise answered with the only word
she could actually say out loud.
And she could say it very, very loudly.
Do you know what that one word was?

"NO!" cried Annalise Devin McFleece. "No, no, NO, no, no!"

"Please take a nap?" begged her father. "Please???"

"NOOOOOO!"

"Excuse me," said a man sitting nearby.

"If she won't take a nap, may I have it, please?"

"I'll also take a nap," said a woman.
"I've had such a busy day. A nap would be
the perfect thing to perk me up!"
And do you know what happened next?

Everybody wanted to take a nap!

The man selling hot dogs.

And the kids playing ball.

And the dog walker walking dogs.

And the baker frosting cookies.

And the construction workers
jackhammering the sidewalk.

And the police officers on patrol.

Even the man who emptied the garbage cans

and the boy on his skateboard

and the girl practicing her juggling.

Yarrrrfff, yawned a big dog stretching out to snooze while two squirrels took a nap in a tree and a mouse took a nap in a pile of leaves.

A flock of pigeons took a nap, *ka-roo, ka-roo, ka-roo*ing— because that's how pigeons snore.

Even the ducks on the pond tucked in their feathers and closed their eyes.

Before long, every single creature in the whole park had decided to take a nap.

But what about Annalise Devin McFleece?

Do you think SHE was taking a nap?

NO!

That's right.
She was the only one in the whole wide
sleepy world who would not fall asleep.

Now there was nothing for Annalise to do.

No one to play with.

No one to fuss, fume, scream, or shriek at.

And all those soft and steady sounds of gentle snoozling?

They made her feel sleepy. Very, very sleepy.
Her eyes grew heavier and heavier.
So heavy, she wanted to take a nap.

But she couldn't.
Because . . .

All the naps had already been taken!

"But I want to take a nap!" shouted Annalise Devin McFleece.

"I WANT TO TAKE A NAP!"

Of course, she didn't really know how to say any of those words, so all that came out was

A "WAAAAAAAH!" so loud, it jounced and jangled and jogged around the park.

(Do you hear it, too?)

But everybody was snoozling so soundly, they didn't even hear it.

Except . . .

AAAAAAAAAA
AAAAAAAAAA
AAAAAAAAAAH!

. . . a gray cat with white paws, napping in a window.

"Meow," said the cat, stretching herself awake. "Don't worry, little girl. Why, I've taken so many naps, I have naps to spare. You can take one of mine."

What happened next, you might wonder?

Well, if you listen closely, you might hear it.

Shhh. Listen.

Can you hear it?

Can you hear all that quiet?

Do you know what that means?

That's right.

Annalise Devin McFleece finally, finally, *finally* took a nap!

Sleep tight!